S0-DSZ-456

Play School ABC

by Rick Bunsen
illustrated by Robbie Stillerman

A GOLDEN BOOK • NEW YORK
Western Publishing Company, Inc., Racine, Wisconsin 53404

Copyright © 1985 by Western Publishing Company, Inc. Illustrations copyright © 1985 by Robbie Stillerman. All rights reserved. Printed in the U.S.A. No part of this book may be reproduced or copied in any form without written permission from the publisher. GOLDEN®, GOLDEN & DESIGN®, A GOLDEN TELL-A-TALE® BOOK, and A GOLDEN BOOK® are trademarks of Western Publishing Company, Inc. Library of Congress Catalog Card Number: 84-72861 ISBN 0-307-07000-X A B C D E F G H I J

A is for Andy. Andy goes to Apple Tree Play School.

B is for bus. *Beep, beep.* The bus takes Andy to play school.

C is for crayons.

D is for desk.

Andy takes his crayons out of his desk and colors a dog.

E is for exercise. Miss Elaine starts each morning with exercise. The class is doing the elephant walk today.

F is for fingers. Andy and his friends paint with their fingers.

G is for garden. Gary and Gail water the garden.

H is for hamsters. Andy feeds Harvey
and Henny, the class pet hamsters.

I is for instrument. At music time, everyone plays an instrument. Ida plays the triangle. D*ing, ding*.

J is for jungle gym. At playtime, Andy
and Jerry swing on the bars.

K is for kite. Miss Elaine helps Kevin and Katie fly a kite.

L is for line. Everyone stands in line to go inside.

M is for mat. Andy rolls out his mat.

N is for nap. The children all take a nap. Zzzz, zzzz.

O is for open. Miss Elaine says, "Time to open your eyes!"

P is for piano. Miss Elaine goes to the piano and plays "The Wake-Up Song."

Q is for quart. Andy pours milk from a quart carton.

R is for raisins. There are round raisin cookies at snack time.

S is for Simon Says. Sally leads the game. She says, "Simon says, stand on your head!"

T is for toy truck. Tina plays with a toy truck till it is time to go home.

U is for umbrella. The children stand under an umbrella while they wait for the bus.

V is for vest. Andy takes off his wet vest.

W is for window. Andy watches out the bus window. Soon he sees his house.

X is for xylophone. After supper, Andy tries to play "The Wake-Up Song" on his toy xylophone.

Y is for yawn. While he is singing, Andy starts to yawn. It's been a busy day.

Z is for zebra. Andy sleeps with Zack, his little toy zebra.

Good night, Andy! Have fun at play
school tomorrow!